Big George

Eric Pringle

illustrated by
Colin Paine

BLOOMSBURY
CHILDREN'S
BOOKS

For Pat, Susannah and David, whose longing
for star worlds is in this story - EP

To Becky - CP

First published in Great Britain in 2001
Bloomsbury Publishing Plc, 38 Soho Square, London, W1D 3HB
This paperback edition first published in 2002

Text copyright © Eric Pringle 2001
Illustrations copyright © Colin Paine 2001
The moral right of the author and illustrator has been asserted

A CIP catalogue record of this book is available from the
British Library

ISBN 0 7475 5544 3

Printed in England by Clays Ltd, St Ives plc

10 9 8 7 6 5 4 3 2 1

contents

Foreword

This book is about England's very first visitor from outer space.

It is the story of how he got his name and how, helped by the smallest of girls, he became the Biggest Hero England Ever Had.

These things happened a long time ago, in the Year of Our Lord 1103.

Close your eyes. Imagine that time ...

The Norman Conquest happened only thirty-seven years ago, and now a Norman, King Henry the First, sits upon the throne of England. He has two and a half million subjects, most of them as poor as church mice.

England is full of dark places. There are deep, dark, trackless forests roamed by deer and wolves and wild boar. There are dark mountain regions where people are afraid to wander and wildcats hiss in the mist. And everywhere the people believe in the dark power of magic, in wizards and witches and the power of potions.

In this half-civilised land, mighty barons hunt in the forests by day, for sport. At night, hungry poachers steal through the trees looking for food.

This is everyday life in the Year of Our Lord 1103.

Nothing extraordinary is happening. But it's about to.

Listen!

Do you hear that noise?

Something is approaching very fast. Heading for England.

Here it comes ...

chapter one
The Stranger

The noise of the crash was heard at court, a hundred miles away.

King Henry looked up, cocked his head and listened for another bang. His courtiers listened too.

When a second tremor did not arrive, Henry nodded wisely and said, 'Meteorite.' (Which was not a bad guess, really.)

His courtiers bowed low and replied, 'Thank you, Your Majesty, for telling us. How wise you are to know such things!'

They all believed it was a meteorite because the King was the King and Kings Know Everything.

Five minutes later the bang was forgotten and Palace life carried on as though nothing had happened.

9

But something *had* happened – something big.

The Stranger had arrived.

Deep in the dark forest, a hundred miles from the King and his courtiers, a machine lay shattered and smoking at the bottom of a vast hole.

Moments earlier it had resembled a shooting star, fire bright, hurtling through Earth's atmosphere in a swizzle of dazzling light. When it smacked into the forest the star went out. Now little green lights fizzed and sparked like glow-worms, and spat puffs of smoke.

Somewhere in the hole, inside the wreckage, in the middle of the sparks, a noise crackled and a panicky voice spluttered gibberish on and off, on and off. Gradually the voice grew fainter, as if it was losing strength, then with a sigh it stopped altogether.

Pieces of the machine lay scattered far and wide among the trees. They too smoked and glowed in the dark night of the forest.

Suddenly the voice returned, screaming. It gave a final command and at once the machine and every scattered piece of metal shone with a blinding light.

Then one by one they shrivelled, the way cotton wool shrinks on a fire, twisting and dwindling until

the machine was no more. The voice died too.

All that was left was a hole in the floor of the
forest, and trees were flattened to twigs all about.

But there was nobody to see these things.

That is how the scene remained for weeks. Still
nobody came to see.

Then one night the silence was broken.

Something stirred in the undergrowth, not far from the hole.

Something had been left after all.

It was big.

It was very big.

If anyone had been watching they would have seen something like an arm raised to scratch what looked like a face – a face covered at its top and bottom with something like hair, only this hair was striped blue and green.

A second arm reached out and pressed against the ground, pushing upright an object that looked very like a body – except that this body was at least as big around and as tall as a tree. The face rose above it and kept on rising. Something like a neck, like a swan's neck that seemed to go on for ever, uncurled slowly and achingly.

As it did so, what sounded like a groan escaped from a mouth hidden inside the blue and green beard. In the silence of the forest the groan sounded as loud as thunder and it made the leaves shiver all around.

Very slowly, with many more groans to make the trees tremble, the whole thing rose up on two enormous legs. Up and up it surged, thrusting through the branches until its head was out in the clear air, towering against the sky and blotting out the stars.

Now at last the Stranger stood upright.

Rocking unsteadily on feet the size of boulders, he looked about him, blinking his eyes in the darkness.

If anyone had been watching they would have thought him the most extraordinary being they had ever seen.

The Stranger was almost human-like, apart from the blue and green hair and the giraffe neck.

Very like and almost a man, but not quite. He was bigger than the biggest tree in the forest. But the oddest thing of all was his face.

It was definitely a face and in many respects it was like a human face. But it was almost white and almost green – a pale greenish white – and it glowed in the dark. It nodded up there against the sky like a full moon.

Actually, it isn't surprising that the Stranger looked like a man in so many ways. Because where he had come from, astronomers had been searching the universe for thousands of years, seeking a star like their own. It was like hunting a needle in a haystack, but in the end they found it.

Earth seemed so similar to their world that those

astronomers thought that everything on it might be similar too. This made them very excited, but it was only guesswork. They had to find out if it really was true.

They decided to send an explorer, a messenger. So they built a spacecraft and aimed it at their discovery, with an astronaut inside – the Stranger.

It worked. Here he was.

But there was an unforeseen problem. The Stranger had no idea who he was, where he was, or what he was doing there.

In the crash of the landing he had been thrown clear of his craft, bumping through the forest and banging his head so hard that now he could not remember anything. And when his craft destroyed itself, there was nothing left to remind him.

He had no past, only a new beginning on an unknown world.

The Stranger had another problem too. He could not get his neck down.

His neck was supposed to fold like a swan's but one of the bumps had locked it fast and now his head was stuck up high and shining like a lamp on a lamp-post.

After teetering on his shaky legs for a while, the Stranger thought he might as well go somewhere, although he had no idea where. So he staggered off, leaving his direction to chance.

As he went, he cut such a swathe through the forest that hunters riding there afterwards thought there must have been a hurricane.

All this a watcher would have seen, if there had been anybody there to see.

And there was.

chapter Two
⌃ Shock For Simpkin Sampkins

There was a poacher.

His name was Simpkin Sampkins, and he was very, very frightened.

Simpkin had pale, watery eyes and no hair and trembling knees. They had been shaking ever since the moment when, setting a rabbit trap, not far away he saw a tree rise up in the darkness and scratch its head.

That had scared Simpkin so much that he almost caught himself in his own trap.

'Jumping fleas in a jam jar!' he muttered, making the sign of a cross on his ragged tunic. 'Bless my toes with honey!'

Simpkin Sampkins lay flat on his back on the

ground, hardly daring to breathe, while what looked like more trees moved and merged into the biggest tree he had ever seen.

'Oh, Mother, forgive me, for I must have been drinking,' he moaned, 'although I don't remember it.'

Gazing at the enormous tree that swayed high above his head, looking as if it might topple on him at any moment, Simpkin began to cry and he began to pray.

He cried that he was sorry for every wicked thing he had ever done. He was sorry for stealing the miller's flour and his daughter Tilly Miller's honey, and for trapping Baron Lousewort's rabbits.

'I will be a poacher no more,' he sobbed. 'And bless my boots with beer but I will never drink alcohol again, for I am being punished with walking trees.'

The Stranger still hovered above him, so Simpkin Sampkins began to pray for a miracle.

'Lord,' he begged, 'if I promise to be good for ever, will you please make this tree go away? *Please?*'

The moment the thought babbled from his brain, the tree moved.

It thumped down a boot as big as a hut, missing Simpkin by a hair and trampling his rabbit trap six feet down into the soft earth.

Next the tree stepped over him and thudded away through the forest, squashing everything in its path.

Simpkin Sampkins lay shivering, rigid as an icicle, for an hour. At last he got up. Peering into the grave where his rabbit trap was buried, he cried again.

Then he ran for his life, watched by a nearby rabbit that rubbed its face with its paws and grinned, glad of its lucky escape.

chapter Three
The Girl at the River

Simpkin Sampkins ran until he thought he could run no more, and still he kept on running. He ran with a stitch in his side and his breath rasping. His legs bled and his hands stung from the briars and nettles that tried to hold him back.

He ran until he reached the edge of the forest and came to the first building on cultivated land. It was a mill, standing sturdily beside the looping bend of a winding river. Simpkin Sampkins had never been so glad to see anything in his life as this mill.

When Simpkin arrived, the night was over and gone. The sun was up and the river shone and the mill-race sparkled as it pushed and dripped over the mill's great turning wheel. The water drove the wheel outside, and the wheel turned, grinding stones inside, and the stones ground corn into flour.

Across the river, inside the mill, Simpkin could hear the miller working beside the noisily grinding millstones, shovelling corn and flour. As he worked, the miller was whistling a happy tune.

Outside, the miller's daughter Tilly was washing his clothes in the river.

The girl was young and small and pretty. She slapped the clothes on flat stones at the water's

edge, and rubbed and shook them. All the time she sang too as she worked, but the song she sang was a sad song.

Tilly looked up from her washing as something appeared out of the forest on the other side of the river.

What she saw looked like a bundle of clothes falling about. It croaked and wobbled and sucked in air. It flapped its arms like wings. Then it sat down and cried.

'Simpkin, is that you?' Tilly shouted.

She carried on washing her father's clothes. She dared not pause because she knew that the miller would have a hundred other things for her to do afterwards.

'Of course it's me!' Simpkin Sampkins wanted to shout back at her. 'Who else would be out in these wild woods at this time in the morning?' But the only sound he could make was a croak like a tired frog.

So he sat on the bank to get his breath back, and looked across the river at Tilly Miller.

Simpkin liked Tilly. He liked watching her. He liked her long yellow hair and the way she tied it back with a band of blue cloth. He liked her smile. He liked the way animals and birds trusted her. That, he knew, was a good sign. They didn't trust *him* as far as they could spit, but that was natural, for he poached them mercilessly.

Simpkin wished Tilly was *his* daughter. He told himself *he* would not work her so hard if she was. He would take care of her far better than that greedy miller, who was so busy making money that he hardly bothered to speak to Tilly, except to give her orders.

And Simpkin knew that if Tilly had been *his* daughter, *he* would not have promised her in marriage to Baron Lousewort's horrible son Bones when she grew up, as her greedyguts father had done. No, sir.

Simpkin had no children.

He had no wife, either.

Simpkin Sampkins had nobody.

People said it was because he was a loner, as if this had been by choice. But Simpkin had not chosen it at all, it was just the way things had worked out.

Whenever he felt lonely Simpkin talked to his friend Tilly. But he had no time to talk to her now because there was a tree on his heels.

Tilly was wringing out the cold washing when finally he came plunging across the river towards her.

'What's up, Simpkin?' she asked.

Simpkin staggered up the beach with water dribbling from his armpits.

'I'm sorry I stole your dad's flour,' he babbled. 'Here, have it back.'

He hauled his poacher's satchel off his back, dragged out a soggy bag and dumped it splat on the ground.

Tilly's blue eyes opened wide with horror. 'Simpkin, how could you!' she cried.

'It was easy,' Simpkin wanted to say, but instead he said, 'And I'm sorry I stole your honey, Tilly.' He pulled out a dripping honeycomb and dropped it squelch on the stones.

'You stole my honey? Why?'

Simpkin wanted to explain that stealing things was what poachers do. But instead his eyes filled with tears. He scratched his bald head. 'I – I'm sorry, Tilly,' he stammered. 'I won't do it again, I promise. Never ever. I've been punished – oh, how I've been punished!'

Tilly examined him closely. 'Simpkin, have you been drinking?'

'Not a drop has touched my lips, Tilly, and never will again. Now I have to go. There's something I must tell people. I have to tell everybody. The forest is alive, and on the move!'

With that he ran away down a track that led

alongside the river to the village, with his arms waving and his bald head bobbing in the sun.

Tilly Miller carried the clean washing into the mill house, where her father was waiting impatiently with a list of jobs for her as long as her arm.

'Simpkin Sampkins is drunk, Father,' Tilly said and smiled. 'He thinks trees are chasing him.'

'Trees will be chasing you if you don't hurry up,' the miller snapped, heading for the door, 'and *I'll* be behind them. I'm off to the village now to deliver flour. If you don't finish that list before I get back you'll be sorry. Understand?'

He banged the door shut behind him without even waiting for his daughter to say yes.

chapter Four
worse than Dragons

The miller did not get far. In fact, he got nowhere at all.

He had just finished harnessing his horse and was loading up the cart with sacks when he heard the sound of hooves.

Looking up he saw a cavalcade of horses approaching along the river track. And what horses they were!

They came trotting up the lane two abreast, fifty, sixty – the miller blinked – there must be a hundred of them at least, he thought. Their teeth gleamed, their eyes flashed, their harnesses jingled and twinkled. Each horse was decked out with coloured saddle-cloth and ribbons and had a rider perched on top, clad from head to foot in dazzling chain mail. The procession glittered like hundreds of mirrors in the early-morning sunshine.

But the miller's heart sank when he saw, bringing up the rear, two horses that were much bigger than the rest. Jerking up and down on them, like two cardboard puppets, were two figures he recognised. They were Baron Grimshanks Lousewort and his weedy son Bones.

The miller swallowed nervously. He guessed what they wanted. The Baron and Bones were coming to look at Tilly, to make sure she was still there. Keeping an eye on their property.

Tilly had also seen them coming, and she too guessed what they wanted. With her heart thumping, she backed into a corner and stood twining her apron strings in her fingers. She wiped a tear from her eye and whispered, 'Oh, please, won't somebody save me from that dreadful boy Bones?' But there was nobody to listen.

When the horsemen arrived, Tilly was kneeling with her face in her hands, praying.

This did her no good at all.

'There's no use pretending this isn't happening, Tilly,' snapped her father, pushing open the door and leading in two of the ugliest, most revolting, nastiest-looking bullies you or England could ever dread to see.

Picture a bursting warty boil with hairs sprouting out at all angles, twisted and wiry and black. Think of a hole in the middle, filled with brown and broken teeth. Now imagine this horror stuck on top of a roly-poly, podgy body like the ugliest balloon in the world.

When you have done this, you will have some idea what Baron Grimshanks Lousewort looked like as he followed the miller into the mill.

Tilly felt sick just to look at him.

She felt even sicker to look at the Baron's son.

Bones Lousewort was thin – thin as a stick insect, thinner than a skeleton – and he looked as if

he didn't have any blood in him. His hands were almost transparent, with pale hooks for fingers. Except for the spots which erupted like a scaly disease all over his skin, his face was white as a sheet. Inside it his eyes glinted like black buttons, his nostrils flared like black holes and his mouth sagged like a dark cave.

Bones looked barely alive.

Worse than that, he looked as if anything he touched would wither too.

And Bones wanted to touch Tilly.

He wanted to hold her hand. He wanted to kiss her. He wanted to *marry* her.

This was because one morning a year ago, returning from a hunting expedition with his father, Bones saw Tilly brushing her long golden hair beside the beehives in front of the mill. He fell for her on sight.

Unfortunately for Bones, no one could possibly fall for him, even though he was the Baron's son and heir and one day would be very rich.

The thought of marrying him filled Tilly with horror and made her want to retch.

Now here he was coming towards her, clicking his stick legs and grinning his death's-head grin.

'Hello, Tilly,' he piped in a thin voice that made the teeth rattle inside his skinny mouth.

Tilly screamed.

'Gadzookles!' growled the Baron, with a grimace that made the hairs jump all over the bursting boil of his face. 'That wench has a good pair of lungs in her. That's a good sign. But you'd better say hello to my son, Tilly, or it will be the worse for your dad, gadzookles in a piecrust if it won't.'

'I will *not* be nice to him!' Tilly shouted. 'I hate him! I can't stand him! I'd rather marry a turnip! Take him away!'

This only made Bones want her more, for although his body was meagre, his skin was as thick as a crocodile's.

But it made the Baron angry and the miller scared.

'Miller!' Grimshanks roared, with his face reddening and swelling until it looked as if it might explode all over the mill. 'If my son wants to marry your daughter he will, gadzookles in a moonbeam if he won't. I'm allowing her to stay here with you only until the time is right, but when I say so you'll hand her over and no messing. Do you understand?'

'I do, my lord,' the miller quaked, and fell to his knees.

The Baron rapped him on the head with his fist. 'If I have any trouble, you'll be out of this mill

faster than you can put your shirt on, and your life won't be worth a fried shrimp. Do you understand *that*?'

'Yes, sir, my lord,' the miller babbled.

The Baron nodded. 'I just hope you do, because

I've had enough nonsense for one day already and it's still only nine o'clock in the morning. We passed that thieving fool Sampkins on the way here, blathering about marching woods. It'll be singing skies next. If Sampkins isn't poaching my game he's drinking himself silly. I gave orders for him to be clapped in jail. That'll cook his goose.'

All this time Bones was smiling at Tilly. His grin struck cold as a knife into her heart.

'Please, Father,' she whispered, 'don't do this to me.'

'Shut up, you, and listen,' the miller hissed back. 'A year ago I promised you to the Baron's son for five sovereigns. Would you have me lose my gold? You'll do exactly as you're told, my girl, and be grateful.'

'Grateful for what?' cried Tilly.

'Grateful for me!' shouted the Baron, coming so close she felt dizzy. The Baron had extremely bad breath.

'Grateful for *me*!' squealed Bones, slithering towards Tilly like a snake. His breath was so nasty it burned like fire.

'Father,' Tilly sobbed, 'this cannot be! These men smell worse than dragons!'

'Dragons!' the Baron roared. 'Ha ha! Ha ha ha!'

'Dragons!' chortled his son.

'Dragons!' chirruped the miller. 'Well, you're intended for this dragon, my girl, so you'd better get used to the smell. What a joke!'

They laughed again, shovelling stench over Tilly like dollops of manure until she fainted clean away.

At that moment, in the trees across the river, something stirred.

Sadie
bookmark

chapter Five
How to Be George

The Stranger had been wandering all night.

He had no idea where he was, even less where he was heading, and where he had been he could not remember. As he wandered, he made a chuntering sound, halfway between a mumbling and a humming, very soft and low. He might have been talking to himself or seeking comfort in a song of home. Who knows?

There was no one to hear him, except the animals who lived in the forest. The noise warned them of his coming so that they were able to skip out of the way and avoid being crushed. The Stranger could not even see where he was going because it was dark.

He had not experienced night before. In the world he had come from it was always day. Its inhabitants stayed awake for the length of nine hundred Earth years, then slept for another nine hundred, silent behind the curtains of their closed eyelids. Which, when you think about it, is almost like living for ever.

The Stranger could not recall any of this, of course. Nor, with his memory gone, could he know that his journey to Earth had lasted eight hundred and ninety-nine years, although he was beginning to feel a little tired.

As he rambled through the forest, he cut a swathe like a maze, which people would spend years trying to get out of afterwards.

At last a new day dawned, and the Stranger began to see where he was.

Then he smelled the river.

He was thirsty and the smell drew him like a magnet, but instinct told him he must be wary. So he got down and crawled along on his great stomach, as carefully as he could between the trees.

When he saw the glint of water ahead, he stopped and pushed out enormous arms to part the undergrowth. Then he probed his giraffe neck about, pushing his head forward until it was just hidden by bushes.

Peering through the twigs, the Stranger saw the river and the mill. And people. Small people!

They seemed to him *very* small people, compared to his own size. Midgets with short necks.

Most of the midgets he saw were sitting on dwarf horses, riding away. The two at the back were laughing. Behind them there trundled a cart laden with sacks, driven by a surly-faced man.

Soon they had all disappeared round the bend of the river.

The Stranger's way seemed clear.

So he crawled out of the bushes and lay down on the beach and drank his fill.

*

Inside the mill, Tilly, who had collapsed only to get rid of the two dragons, decided she had lain still long enough. It was time to start the jobs her father had left her. She jumped to her feet and looked at the daunting list.

She was to seek wood from the forest and chop it.

She was to fetch water from the river and boil it on the fire.

She was to clean the house and set the mousetraps.

She was to cook dinner.

And so on.

Etcetera.

There was no end to the work.

Tilly sighed, but she knew that sighing wouldn't help and so there was no point doing it. The only thing to do was make a start and tick the jobs off one by one.

So she picked up a pail and opened the door and went outside to collect water from the river.

And that was when she saw it.

She saw Whatever It Was, spreadeagled on the bank, stretching out of the forest to halfway across the river, guzzling.

'By George,' Tilly exclaimed in an astonished voice, 'you're big! You're *very* big, by George.'

Whatever It Was lifted its head at the sound.

Water streamed in rivulets from its blue and green beard.

'By *George*,' Tilly said again, 'has someone been painting you?'

The ears of the Whatever It Was twitched. It seemed to be concentrating. Its eyes glittered. Its mouth formed a shape, and, making a chuntering sound like a soft, low humming, it said, slowly and carefully, 'G-g-g-e-e-e-o-o-o-r-r-r-g-g-e.'

Tilly was a bright girl. Not a lot passed her by, and she was an athlete at jumping to conclusions.

'Is that your name?' she asked. 'Is it George, by George? What a coincidence!'

The Stranger smiled the biggest smile Tilly had ever seen. She was on a level with its teeth and from where she stood its mouth looked as if it could swallow the world.

The Stranger was smiling at Tilly's bright musical voice. It sounded friendly. It was the first friendliness he had come across since he found himself lying on the floor of the forest, a Stranger without a history.

'I'm Tilly,' the very small person across the river was saying now. 'How do you do?'

'T-illllll-llll-yyy.'

'That's right. Want to shake hands?' Tilly held out her hand.

39

George pushed himself up on one elbow, making a wave that surged out of sight down the river. Then he stretched out his other arm towards her.

And stretched.

And stretched.

The arm seemed to be made of elastic. It kept coming until it was within a hair's breadth of her face. Then it stopped. Tilly, who was not a girl to scare easily, grasped a finger in both hands and shook it.

'Pleased to meet you, George,' she said, smiling.

The Stranger liked her smile. He liked the way it lit up her face. He grinned back.

'Hello,' he said. In his own language.

To Tilly it sounded like 'G-r-o-l-y-h-o-o-m-p', and straight away she raced to another conclusion.

'Is that what you are?' she asked. 'A grolyhoomp? Do you know, I've never met a grolyhoomp in the whole of my life before! I've never even heard of one, by George!'

chapter six
Listening to the Sky

If you are thinking that Tilly is taking this very casually, remember that it is happening in the Year of Our Lord 1103, when people believe absolutely in every kind of wonder. And if you believe in fairies and witches and boggarts and goodness knows what else, why not in a grolyhoomp?

Actually, Tilly was very excited, because it isn't every day a girl gets to meet a grolyhoomp. In fact, she had never heard of anyone meeting one before.

But it is one thing finding a grolyhoomp outside your door and quite another knowing what to do with it. That is what Tilly was pondering now.

'Excuse me for asking, George,' she said very politely, 'but would you mind getting out of the river? You're making a dam and in about five minutes my father's mill will be flooded. *If* you don't mind. Thank you so much.'

Although he had no idea what the words meant – it sounded to him like a kind of melody – George seemed to understand.

He stood up.

And up.

Waterfalls cascaded from his armpits and the holes in his tunic, soaking Tilly from head to foot as in two strides he crossed the river and stood towering above her.

She looked up at him until her neck ached. Blinking at the bright stripy face perched on top of that long neck, she said, 'Oh, George, you must be forty feet high!'

The grolyhoomp grinned down and repeated, 'F-f-f-o-o-r-r-t-i-f-f-y. Four-t-i-fy.'

'Close,' said Tilly. 'You're getting there.'

But she was thinking, Now what?

Because up to now, conversation didn't seem to be getting them very far, and at this rate her father would be back before she had even started on her chores. Then she would be for it.

Tilly thought hard. What on earth was she going to do with Big George? (It never occurred to her to wonder what Big George might be going to do with her.)

She could hardly take him visiting. Try as she might she could not see herself turning up at a friend's house and saying, 'Look, I've just found this forty-foot grolyhoomp called George. Can I bring him in for tea?'

In the end she decided that the best way through the puzzle was to be logical. To put things in order. First things first. And the first priority was to get those jobs out of the way.

'Why don't you go round the back and hide, George?' she suggested. 'Make yourself scarce for a bit. I'll hurry my chores and when I've finished, I'll come round for a chat. How does that sound?'

It sounded like magic to George – all jiggy and sing-songy, like the kind of music that makes your feet tap. It made him happy to hear it.

So, chuntering gently, he followed Tilly's pointing finger and wandered round to the back of the mill.

Here trees had been cleared to make a wide yard where the miller stored grain at harvest time. Now in spring most of the grain had been ground into flour and sold and the clearing was almost empty.

George lay down in the open space. He stretched out and waited for Tilly.

He had to wait for a long time.

He felt tired, though not sleepy, for it was not yet his time to sleep. His nine hundred years of waking were not quite used up.

His neck was bruised and stiff. A bump on the back of his head felt as big as his boot. He touched it gently and groaned.

He tried to think things out, but that made his head ache even more, so he stopped.

To take his mind off his troubles, George thought about Tilly. That did not hurt, because he liked her. He wanted to be her friend.

He practised her language so that they could talk to each other. 'G-e-o-o-r-r-g-e,' he hummed. 'Ff-o-rrt-i-fy.'

(Tilly, hurrying through the chores on her list, heard the sound inside the mill and thought her bees were all swarming at once.)

Now George lay back and looked straight up at the sky.

Fleecy clouds floated across it like fish swimming in a blue sea.

But there was something strange.

The sky was singing.

George strained to listen, but could make no sense of it. It seemed to him that he should be able to look through the clouds and see what lay beyond, but trying to do that made his head ache again, and failing to do it made him want to cry with loneliness.

The sky seemed like a friend calling him, but he couldn't quite hear it, and he could not answer.

He tried to imitate the sound, opening his lips and whistling. His whistling was a wind that shook the branches of the trees all around the clearing. Birds flew startled from their nests. Insects scurried

and darted into holes. Miles away, owls hooted with surprise.

Inside the mill Tilly heard a hurricane.

Where on earth did that come from? she wondered. I hope George is all right.

The wind dropped as suddenly as it rose. Everything grew hushed and still. Breathless.

In the clearing George was crying.

chapter Seven
The Tilly Bird

Even though she worked her very quickest, when Tilly had finished her tasks, the day was already ending. Her father must be home soon.

She felt tired and frightened and sad. The Baron's visit had reminded her of the fate she had been trying hard to forget, for just the idea of being married to Bones Lousewort was more than she could bear. She felt like running away, but there was nowhere for her to run to.

The worry was still on Tilly's mind when at last she was able to visit the grolyhoomp.

She paused at the rim of the clearing and looked at him. The very sight of George cheered her up, he was so astonishing. He nearly filled the clearing all by himself. With that amazing neck, his striped, tufty hair and beard, his elastic arms and knobbly

hands and boulder-sized feet, he hardly looked real.

But he was real all right. Why, he was turning his head towards her now, and smiling!

What a smile that was! It wafted over her like a blanket. It warmed her up. It comforted her.

But even so, she still felt sad.

George saw her pain and frowned. 'What's the matter, Tilly?' he asked.

Tilly heard, 'Trlllleddibbbileppolyubftsatilly,' which made no sense whatever. Yet the sound comforted her because it was so friendly.

She moved up close and looked the grolyhoomp in the eye. That brought another surprise, for it was like looking into a deep black pool in which she could see herself swimming.

Tilly had the strangest feeling that she had swum right inside the grolyhoomp's head. She felt sure he was inside hers, too.

It was like being best friends with somebody, so close that you each know what the other is feeling. Tilly thought there wasn't anything about her that George could not guess and understand.

So she poured out her troubles. She told him about her life and her father's promise to the Baron.

'I'm too small to marry, aren't I?' she cried. 'Look

at me, I'm a midget. It makes me scared to grow up, thinking about that skinny bonebag waiting for me with his smelly breath. Bones is a monster! One puff from him and I'll die! I know I shall!'

George winked and jumped to his feet, making the trees shiver and the ground tremble.

Tilly nearly fell over.

'You're not going away?' she cried.

George was not going anywhere. He had something else in mind.

He had understood not one word from his small friend, but the sound of her voice had moved him like sad music. How unhappy she was!

Well, he was going to make her happy.

From his great height he looked down on the top of Tilly's head. She looked very tiny and delicate. He would have to be careful.

'Larklyggwocavvuiotpvnmjnms,' he said. It meant, 'Watch this.'

Slowly, like a giraffe nibbling short grass, he spread wide his legs, bent his long neck and lowered his head to the ground.

Once again his eye was level with Tilly's, and once again she saw herself inside it.

'Ffffbbiggley,' he said. He waggled his head. 'Ffffbbiggley!'

'You want me to climb up?' Tilly gasped.

'Mmmnnn. MMMnnn!'

'All right, George. If you say so.'

She grabbed hold of the grolyhoomp's tufty beard. It felt like a handful of wire.

'Blue and green should never be seen, George,' she said. 'That's a basic rule of colours. But I expect grolyhoomps haven't been taught – wheeee!'

George lifted his head and Tilly swooped upwards. With legs dangling she hung on to the wiry beard with all her strength.

'Wheee!' she shouted again as George straightened his neck and back and brought his legs together.

She was swinging back and forth like the pendulum of a giant clock. Trees and sky rocked dizzily about her.

Then her kicking feet found a hold on George's bottom lip. 'Is that all right?' she asked breathlessly. 'I'm not hurting you?'

'Qqqwwallopmid,' George laughed, and Tilly bounced up and down.

Now that she felt safer, she dared to look about. What she saw made her cry out with excitement. 'George, this is the most wonderful thing I ever did!'

Suddenly she was no longer a miller's daughter, promised in marriage to a dragon.

She was a bird. A bird flying above the treetops.

Tilly had never seen the tops of trees before. It was amazing, like looking down on enormous cushiony mushrooms.

She laughed out loud. She was a bird soaring in a blue sky, so high she felt that she only had to reach out to touch the clouds.

Then George began to turn and now she was a bird winging above the mill and the shining river. Far below the turning waterwheel splashed a million sparkling diamonds of water. On the river, swans with necks like George's swam like little stately boats. Tiny cows grazed the fields. From up here she could see how the river ran, on through field and forest towards the village where her father lingered.

Now Tilly heard a strange noise. It was like humming, a deep strong droning somewhere between a shout and a murmur. It made the air tingle and it made Tilly feel very happy.

George was singing.

Then, shockingly, the world moved.

It went down and up and down again, and up and down and up, faster and faster. Trees rocked before her eyes. The sky lurched.

Holding tightly to George's beard, Tilly rose

and fell and spun and swung until she hardly knew
where she was.

George was dancing.

He danced and sang and the world whirled and Tilly shouted for joy.

George heard her and laughed. His plan had worked.

As dusk fell, the girl and the grolyhoomp jumped about in the forest clearing and were happy.

That is how they were when the miller saw them.

chapter Eight
Nightmares

The miller had delivered all his flour by the middle of the morning. Then, because his daughter was taking care of all the work at home, he went to the alehouse.

And stayed there.

He drank some ale.

He drank some more ale.

Villagers trickled in and out of the alehouse during the day. The miller drank with them all, and told each one how he was to be related to the Baron, because his daughter was going to marry the Baron's only son.

'I'm celebrating,' he said. 'Have some ale.'

'Have some more ale.'

The day grew hot.

At three o'clock in the afternoon the miller

staggered out of the alehouse. Across the shimmering dusty square he spotted Simpkin Sampkins watching him through the bars of the jail.

'You'll never get my daughter, you putrid poaching piewacket!' the miller shouted. 'She's for Bones-Worse-Than-a-Dragon!'

Roaring at his joke, the miller reeled back into the alehouse.

A tear rolled down Simpkin Sampkins's cheek.

When the miller had spent all his money, the sun

had sunk low in the sky. By this time he was so drunk he could no longer stand up.

So somebody brought his horse. Somebody else fetched his cart. Somebody connected the horse to the cart and somebody else carried the miller out of the alehouse and dumped him in it.

Then all four somebodies shouted, 'Go home!' to the horse, and watched the cart trundle away with the miller snoring noisily on top.

Then they turned to each other and said how sorry they felt for Tilly, and wasn't it a pity that nothing could be done about it, because the Baron's word was law.

Simpkin Sampkins heard them.

'If I was out of this jail,' he said to himself, '*I* would do something about it. Though I don't know what, just at this moment.'

The horse pulled the cart and the cart carried the miller towards his mill, along the track beside the river.

Evening had arrived and the light was fading fast. Midges nipped the miller's face. Bats zipped past his ears.

Although the miller could hardly hear anything because of the noise of ale sloshing in his stomach, and although he could hardly see because of the dying light and the pink mist which had formed in front of his eyes, as the cart neared his mill he thought …

He certainly thought …

He was almost sure …

Was there singing?

Was there laughing?

And what on earth was that huge shape bobbing against the sky above the mill roof, with a midget dangling from it?

The miller shut his eyes. Was it something … or nothing?

He opened his eyes again and the shapes were still there. Dancing.

The miller's heart turned upside down. His stomach slipped sideways.

'Mother,' he moaned, 'I'm seeing things!'

Then the good horse stopped outside its stable and the miller stared up from the cart at his worst nightmare.

Out of it his daughter's voice cried, 'Hello, Dad! Look at me!'

With a cry of fear the miller staggered to his feet and fell off the cart.

By the time Tilly reached him he was snoring again, fast asleep beside the waterwheel which was churning water all over him.

Tilly helped her father to his bed. She took off his boots and covered him with a blanket, praying that when he woke he would remember nothing of what he had seen. Because if he did, there would be trouble.

There was always trouble where the miller was. He was that sort of man.

When this last weary task of the day was done, Tilly headed for bed herself. She was very tired. It had been a hard day and a strange day, but it had ended up being the most exciting day of her life.

Tilly slept on a heap of old sacks at the very top of the mill. As she climbed up the stairs towards it, she paused to look through a window. She rubbed away dust and cobwebs and peered out into the night.

In the dim starlight she could just make out the line of trees where the forest began behind the mill. Low down beneath the branches a pale light glimmered, as if the moon had come down to Earth and was resting on the ground for a while.

'Goodnight, Big George,' she whispered.

The Stranger lay across the clearing. Unfamiliar darkness covered him, except where the glow from his face cast a ghostly pallor on the ground beside his head.

He was looking at the sky and listening. The stars were singing.

The Stranger did not know why this should be, but he felt the music run through his veins and into his heart.

It haunted him.

chapter Nine
Sludge, Bog and Grolyhoomp

In the morning Tilly rose early.

She knew that this day she must set the mill grinding herself, because when her father finally woke he would have an ache in his head like a blacksmith's hammer thumping an anvil, and a moan in his mouth like a bleating sheep. He would be useless for hours.

This had happened many times before.

Tilly had another reason to be about early. She wanted to see her grolyhoomp again.

Still excited by that amazing dance, she sang as she washed her face in a bucket of cold water and brushed her long hair.

She was singing as she ran down the stairs, but when she entered the milling floor, the song died on her lips. Somebody had risen even earlier than she.

Two somebodies.

They were standing on the millstone like warts on legs, waiting for her.

Silas Sludge and Bartholomew Bog were as alike as two peas from a very nasty pod. They were short and leery and the skin of their faces was like wrinkled paper, furrowed into scowls and frowns and grimaces. Both had pointy noses and pointy feet and pointy hands.

The only difference between them, the only way you could tell them apart, was this.

Silas Sludge had crafty, slidy, slippy, grey eyes that were hard as stones and mean as mousetraps.

Bartholomew Bog had rolling, yellow, jaundiced eyes that were never still. He looked like a fever in motion and he was as prim and sniffy as a pedigree cat.

They were bad news, as vile and pitiless a pair of characters as you could ever dread to meet on a dark night, and they looked even worse perched on a millstone pointing their sharp fingers at you at six o'clock on a spring morning.

The Sludge was Baron Lousewort's steward. The Bog was the Baron's bailiff. They were always together, but you could not say they were friends because they were always arguing.

'Don't point your fingers at me, it's rude,' Tilly

said when she had got over the surprise of seeing them there.

'*I* wasn't pointing, *he* was,' said Bog, pointing at Sludge.

'No, he wasn't, *I* was,' Sludge argued, pointing back. For a moment he looked doubtful, as if something wasn't quite right, but he changed the subject and said, 'The Baron sent us.'

'He sent me,' said the Bog.

'No, he didn't, he sent you,' snapped Silas.

The warts moved around their faces like counters.

'What didn't he send you for?' Tilly asked.

'To keep an eye on you, that's what,' Bartholomew sniffed. He was manicuring his nails with a stick and his eyes rolled with concentration.

'To report on your doings,' hissed Silas, stepping off the millstone and waddling across the dusty floor to Tilly. He stopped just in front of her, glared at her with his slippy eyes and pointed a jabbing finger into her face. '*That's* what.'

'No, it isn't,' said the Bog.

'And what's more,' growled the Sludge, 'we're to stay here and watch you until you marry Master Bones.'

'No, he isn't, *we* are,' corrected the Bog.

Tilly's heart sank. If these two horrors were going to spy on her every minute – and she knew they would, right up to the moment Bones Lousewort slipped a ring on her finger – how would she be able to see George?

How would she have any freedom?

It would be worse than being in prison, and with a life sentence waiting at the end of it.

Bartholomew Bog swayed forward to stand

shoulder to shoulder with Silas Sludge. They were both so close that Tilly could see the red veins snaking across their eyes, the hairs sprouting out of their noses and the dirt in the nails of the fingers that stabbed the air in front of her.

She screamed with fright.

Tilly was never certain exactly what happened after that, because she had her back to the mill door and Silas and Bartholomew were facing it. All she knew was that one minute they were threatening her and the next they were whimpering, backing away with eyes popping and warts leaping like jumping beans.

'Take it away!' babbled Bog.

'*You* take it!' gabbled Sludge.

'No, *you*!'

'Yes, me – no, not me, *you*!'

Tilly turned to look and saw an arm, massive as a tree trunk, filling the doorway. From its hand a huge finger probed. The finger was moving across the floor, pointing, pushing and hopping like a leg towards the intruders.

'Aaahh!' screamed the steward.

'Aaahh!' yelled the bailiff.

For once they were in agreement, but it was much too late.

The finger flicked.

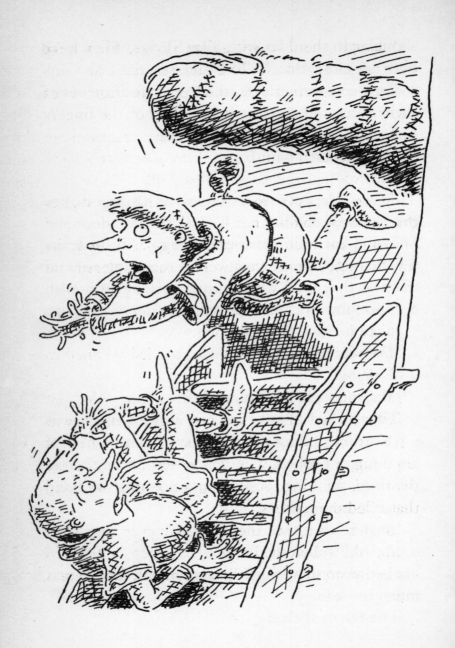

It caught them square on and flipped them head over heels towards the back stairs.

Down they tumbled, waving their short arms and yelling.

At the bottom they picked themselves up and ran for their lives, bursting to tell the Baron about the Great Pointing Finger of Tilly's Mill.

Their tale, and the finger, would get bigger every time they told it.

Inside the mill another door opened and the miller staggered through. He gazed blearily at Tilly.

'Did I hear a noise?' he asked.

Then he saw the finger.

It looked as big as his horse, and it beckoned to him. *Beckoned*.

The miller's face turned to ashes. 'No,' he whispered. 'Oh, no. Please, no.' He closed his eyes.

When he opened them again, it was no better. If anything, it was worse, for now he could have sworn his daughter was sitting on a hand – a hand that filled the mill. *His* mill.

'Slap me with an elephant if I ever touch ale again,' the miller whimpered, staggering back to his bedroom and shutting the door firmly behind him.

*

'Now look what you've done, George,' Tilly Miller said, smiling at the dark shining eye beyond the doorway.

The eye winked at her and a deep voice hummed.

'Grolyhoomp,' it said.

She understood that he meant, 'Good morning, Tilly.'

chapter Ten
The walking Tree

As Silas Sludge and Bartholomew Bog hurried towards Lousewort Castle, which stood on a hill high above the village, an extraordinary noise came sounding towards the mill.

When Tilly heard it she was frightened, for already it was too close to give her time to hide George.

The noise was made up of many different sounds, all borne along the river on the morning breeze.

There was a sound of men talking and shouting.

There was a sound of women and children laughing and singing as if they were going to a fair.

There was a sound of dogs barking.

There was a sound of cats miaowing.

There was a sound of tramping feet, as if the whole village was marching to the mill.

Above all this Tilly heard Simpkin Sampkins's squeaky voice.

'I *did* see it,' he was shouting. 'A walking tree! I saw a whole forest on the move! Wait until *you* see it, you won't believe your eyes!'

The moment Simpkin Sampkins had been freed from jail he had told his story to anyone who would listen. And just about *everybody* had listened, as you would if somebody offered to show you a walking wood.

Now the villagers were coming to see this miracle for themselves.

Tilly gave George a brave smile.

'Stand up, Mr Grolyhoomp,' she said and gestured.

Her voice was sweet as a violin to George's ears. He smiled back at her and rose up like a tower in front of the mill.

Tilly stationed herself in front of his feet, folded her arms and waited.

George folded his arms too.

They stood very still.

'This way!' they heard Simpkin Sampkins shout. 'This way to the place where trees run and branches fly!'

Around the bend of the river they came, Simpkin swinging his arms in front, the people marching behind and the dogs and cats running about their feet.

And they saw.

Their mouths fell open.

They stopped in their tracks.

They saw Tilly Miller, but she was no surprise because they knew her already. The surprise was the thing behind her.

Behind and above her.

Way above her.

When they saw the thing, they laughed.

It's a curious fact that when people come up against something they don't understand, they either laugh at it or they fear it. Or both.

If they fear it they hate it for scaring them, and attack it.

And when they laugh at it, they often attack it too.

That is what happened now.

When the villagers found their voices again, they turned to Simpkin Sampkins and demanded, 'Is *that* your marching tree?'

Simpkin wasn't sure, but he decided to make the most of it. 'Didn't I tell you!' he squealed, looking so wild with his wide, watery eyes and shining, bald head that somebody began to snigger.

Then they all laughed together, and snorted, 'What's that stripy turnip, Tilly? Does it *do* anything? Does it *say* anything? Is it *real*?'

'Say something, George,' Tilly murmured.

The Stranger gazed down at the giggling people. He supposed that since they were Tilly's people they too must be friendly, so he smiled happily and opened his enormous mouth and slowly and carefully spoke the words he had learned from her.

'Ggg-e-e-o-o-r-r-r-g-g-e,' he said. 'Ffo-r-r-rtti-fy.'

'What's that?'

The villagers frowned and muttered to each other.

'What did it say?'

'What was that all about? George fortify? Fortify George?'

'What does it mean?'

'The thing must be an idiot.'

Big George grinned. 'Grolyhoomp,' he said, though he meant, 'Hello'.

'Grolyhoomp!' they laughed.

'Grolyhoomp!' they sneered.

'George is a grolyhoomp,' Tilly explained gently, 'and my friend.'

The villagers roared, but when George did not say anything else or do anything else, their laughter grew bored and bad-tempered.

'We don't want strangers here,' snarled the fat barmaid from the alehouse who had served the miller with ale all the previous day.

'Especially grolyhoomps!' snapped the alehouse keeper. 'He'll drink us dry!'

He threw a stone at George.

That began it.

Suddenly the villagers were all snatching stones from the river bank and hurling them at the grolyhoomp. They bounced off him like peanuts.

'Stop it!' Tilly screamed.

She ran to stop them but the fat woman grabbed her by the shoulders and turned her round.

'Tell that thing to go away!' she hissed. 'Whatever it is, we don't want it here. Tell it to go away!'

Tilly looked up at George.

George looked down at Tilly.

Although the stones were not hurting him he could see that these people were angry. Their voices were harsh and unpleasant, quite unlike Tilly's.

And Tilly was crying now.

George stooped to her.

'Spriglerwkaiytebiooltilly,' he said, meaning, 'Don't cry, Tilly.'

At his movement the villagers shrank back. Now they had laughed and thrown their stones they didn't know what to do next.

'What did he say?' a man shouted.

'Spriggle something,' a lame, ragged woman replied. She waved her stick at George.

'Kityboothingy,' a boy yelled. 'Or something.'

As they stood scowling and muttering, George leaned low and touched Tilly's cheek, wiping away her tear with his finger.

'Friend,' he said in his own language.

One word.

It made no sense to anyone else, but Tilly understood.

She sniffed.

'George,' she said, and smiled through her crying, 'you're a big softy.'

Watching the grolyhoomp and the girl smiling at each other made the people restless. They wanted action. They wanted something to happen.

And something did happen.

In fact, *three* things happened very quickly, all of them bad.

chapter Eleven
OFF With HiS HeaD!

The first thing happened when George looked up and saw a tiny shape circling high in the blue sky.

All at once it dropped like a stone and landed on his head.

A crow.

The crow cawed and flapped its black shiny wings. It shuffled about as if making a nest in George's striped hair, and settled down.

'Grolyhoomp,' said George.

'Caw,' said the crow.

The villagers didn't like this one little bit, because it looked like a sign. In those superstitious days people looked for signs or portents everywhere, and crows were signs *and* portents. Crows were bad luck.

It followed that a crow making itself at home on a grolyhoomp's head meant that the grolyhoomp must be bad luck too.

They backed further off and murmured anxiously among themselves. What they murmured amounted to one thing: the grolyhoomp must be got rid of, fast.

But how?

The grolyhoomp was big, very big. It was much too big for them to deal with. They would need help.

That was when the second thing happened. The miller opened his window and looked groggily out at the morning.

As his throbbing eyes looked from left to right, this is what he saw.

First he saw what looked like the entire population of the village huddled by the river, whispering.

The miller didn't like the look of that.

Then he saw that all the dogs and cats of the neighbourhood were there too, frozen like statues with their eyes on stalks and their hair standing on end.

The miller liked that even less. That looked scary.

But it was nothing to the sight that hit his eyes next.

He saw his daughter sitting with her arms folded on the biggest boot he had ever seen. Above the boot was the biggest leg, and above the leg was the biggest body, and above the body was the longest neck, and at the end of the neck was the oddest-looking head you could imagine, striped blue and green.

On the top sat a crow, like a black cherry on a cake.

'Oh, my,' said the miller.

He blinked. Twice.

'Oh, my,' he said again. 'I'm still drunk. I've never been this drunk before.'

As he hung out of the window, the miller prayed that he *was* drunk and that none of this was real.

He was disappointed.

'Good morning, Father,' his daughter called.

'Grolyhoomp,' said the giant with the crow on his head.

'Oh, my,' the miller groaned. 'Oh, my, oh, my, oh, my.'

He started to cry.

Just then thundering hooves, and shouts, and a jingling of harness could be heard. And that was the beginning of the third thing happening.

This third item was very bad news for George.

Into sight galloped a dozen horses. Eight carried soldiers, two bore Silas Sludge and Bartholomew Bog, and the last two brought the Baron and Bones Lousewort.

Silas Sludge and Bartholomew Bog were waving their arms and squealing excitedly. They had not stopped squawking since, puffing and blowing, they had reached the Baron's castle and poured out their incredible story.

They were still pouring, and the Baron was heartily sick of it.

'Finger big as the world,' croaked his steward, who was growing hoarse.

'Not at all,' argued his bailiff, in a piping squeak which was all the voice he had left. 'Big as the sky.'

'Bigger,' croaked Sludge.

'Bigger than everything there is,' squeaked Bog.

'Bigger that that.'

'Bigger, bigger, bigger.'

'Shut up!' yelled the Baron.

It was only to stop their nonsense that he had agreed to come on this fool's errand.

'If you don't stop gabbling,' he threatened, 'I'll cut out your tongues and swap them over.'

The thought of each having the other's tongue and arguing with himself to the end of time closed their mouths tight.

But then the mill came into sight, and the Baron saw what he saw.

He saw the miller hanging out of his window and he saw all his people white as ghosts, and he saw Tilly and he saw ...

'Oh, my,' the Baron said.

'What did we tell you?' said the Sludge and the Bog. They spoke with their mouths closed, so that it sounded like, 'Waaaaaaaaaiiieeeeeeoooo' – which is exactly what the Baron was thinking.

But the Baron wasn't a baron for nothing. He

pulled himself up and pulled up his horse. Then he said, very politely for him, 'Good morning, Tilly.'

'Good morning, Baron,' said Tilly.

She looked very small and very determined.

'Hello, Tilly,' said Bones, baring his teeth in a smile like sick in a bucket.

Tilly gave him a stare which would have melted him off his horse if he hadn't been so dense.

'Come here, Tilly,' ordered the Baron.

'No,' said Tilly.

'Do as you're told.'

Tilly folded her arms tighter and said, 'Why don't you come and make me?'

The villagers gasped, because nobody ever argued with the Baron and lived.

The Baron swelled with fury, for even his highest noblemen did not dare to speak to him like that. Yet here was this chit of a girl … he'd have to sort her out.

But maybe not just at this moment.

'What's *that*?' he asked instead.

'He's a grolyhoomp,' explained Tilly.

'Yours, is he?'

'I think he belongs to himself,' Tilly said.

'Don't be cheeky.'

The Baron rode a few careful paces forward, then stopped and gazed up at George.

'Look here, you,' he snarled. 'I am Baron Grimshanks Lousewort of Lousewort Castle. Get that?'

'G-e-e-o-o-r-r-g-g-e,' said George.

'And you are George. All right. Well, George, this is my land and you can't stay on it, so clear off. And, ahem, I'd go quietly if I were you, get my meaning?'

While he was talking, the Baron was eyeing the

grolyhoomp and calculating how much he would eat in a day.

'By George,' he said to himself, 'he'll eat me out of house and home! In a week I'll have no cows or milk left. In two weeks he'll clear me out of pigs and sheep and rabbits and rivers. In three weeks I'll be starving. Well, I'm not having that, thank you very much.'

Frowning, he rode back to his men. 'Chase it away,' he ordered. 'Clear the grolyhoomp out of my territory.'

'Don't even think about it!' Tilly shouted. But

she was growing anxious, for the villagers had lined up behind the soldiers and there seemed such a lot of them against one gentle grolyhoomp.

It wasn't fair.

'Well, get on with it!' the Baron barked, making Bones jump in his saddle.

The soldiers rode a few paces forward, then stopped. Their horses refused to go any further, for which disobedience the soldiers were deeply grateful. None of them was keen to be within grolyhoomp range.

The Baron saw their reluctance and snarled, 'All

right, kill him instead. You can do that long distance.'

'No!' screamed Tilly. 'Don't you dare!'

'Yes!' shouted the villagers. 'Finish him! Off with his blue and green head!'

Tilly looked at George with tears in her eyes and put her arms around as much of his leg as she could manage.

'I'd get out of the way if I was you,' said the Baron with an evil chuckle. 'Unless you want to be splattered as well, of course.'

He squinted at his men.

'Are you ready?' he snapped. 'Right, then. Ready, steady ...'

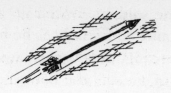

chapter Twelve
A Marriage is Arranged

George was no fool. He knew there was a problem. So he leaned down towards the little squirt on a horse who was doing all the talking and said, 'Hifflethwackserrumptermiff.' Meaning, 'Push off.'

'Beg pardon?' said the Baron, astonished. The hum of George's voice echoed round his eardrums and he had to smack the side of his head to get rid of it. 'Say that again?'

'Ticktockthwackyrote,' George said, meaning, 'I'm warning you.'

'That's just nonsense,' the Baron snorted. 'I won't listen to it.'

Once more he turned to his men.

'Kill him again,' he commanded. 'Kill him twice! Three times if you like.'

But when the soldiers looked up at George, he did not seem quite so friendly as he had before. So instead of advancing, they backed away.

'You bunch of sneaks!' the Baron screamed. 'You panload of cowardy custards! I'll have you shovelling manure for the rest of your days, see if I won't!'

He was so worked up the warts on his face squirmed like ferrets. But when he turned to his son, he smiled encouragingly.

'*You* do it, Bones,' he said. 'Show these jellies how it's done.'

Bones turned a paler shade of white. 'Do I have to, Dad?'

'Of course you do. This is your chance to show Tilly what you're made of.'

'But I feel sick, Dad.'

The Baron foamed at the mouth. 'Is everybody in the world useless?' he ranted. 'I'll give gold to the first man who rids me of this – this *thing*!'

'Hang on!' the miller shouted from his upstairs window. 'I'm coming down!'

The villagers had forgotten all about him, but now they remembered that this miller was the greediest man alive. Why, he would do anything for money, even sell his daughter to a dragon.

So they weren't surprised when he ran among them piping, 'I'll do it! Let me do it!'

'You wouldn't dare, Father!' Tilly screamed.

'Mind your own business, you,' her father hissed. 'You should be getting on with your work, not hugging boots.'

Borrowing a bow and arrow from the nearest soldier, he walked forward, craned his neck, squinted and took aim at George.

'Cover your face, George!' Tilly shouted. 'Guard your eyes!'

George raised his hands, but too late. The arrow bounced off his nose. It hurt.

'Ow,' George said.

'I understood that!' the Baron shouted, jumping up and down for joy. 'I understood a grolyhoomp! Well done, that miller. Kill him some more!'

Now the miller collected a whole sheaf of arrows.

The soldiers, noticing that the miller was still alive, grew bolder and fitted arrows into their bows too.

The villagers also grew brave and gathered stones.

Silas Sludge and Bartholomew Bog loaded catapults.

The Baron drew his sword.

Bones sucked in air and breathed it out again.

This was all too much for Tilly. She knew what

would happen. In her imagination she saw the arrows thudding into George's eyes and the stones flying into his face, and his blood spurting.

He would be hurt, and he was too gentle to fight back.

Tilly couldn't bear it.

She ran into the river, shouting, 'Follow me, George!'

George hesitated.

'Come on!' Tilly pleaded. 'Hurry! Please hurry!'

She swam through the water and climbed up the opposite bank.

Just as the arrows were released and the stones thrown, George turned to follow.

The crow flew away squawking and the weapons bounced harmlessly off George's back as he forded the river and followed Tilly into the forest.

Soon they had both vanished from sight, although for a long time the people at the mill could hear undergrowth crashing and trees splintering. Then that, too, faded away.

'That's got rid of him!' cried the Baron with a self-satisfied smirk. 'He won't come back here in a hurry.' Then he shouted, 'Go home, everybody! The fun is over. Get back to your work!'

Now only the Baron and Bones and the miller were left standing there.

'I want Tilly,' Bones whimpered.

'Stop snivelling,' the Baron snapped. 'You'll have her sooner than you think.'

He frowned at the miller. 'That does it, miller,' he said. 'We've waited long enough.'

The miller was feeling that if he did not get his hands on some gold soon, he would burst.

'So have I,' he grumbled. 'When do I get my money for seeing off that grolyhoomp?'

'The only time you'll see gold,' said the Baron, 'will be when my son marries your daughter. It had better be soon, too, because I've had just about enough of her disobedience and cheek.'

'All right,' said the miller. 'He can have her tomorrow. I'll see to it personally.'

'Done,' said the Baron, spitting on his hands and slapping them across the miller's face. 'A promise is a promise, mind. If you don't keep it, you die.'

'I'll keep it!' the miller cried.

Now at last they were all happy.

Grinning with satisfaction, the Baron and his bony offspring rode away.

The miller watched them depart. As soon as they were out of sight, he ran into his mill, dancing and singing with happiness at the thought of the pieces of gold he could already feel in his hand.

Seconds later Simpkin Sampkins emerged from where he had hidden himself behind the waterwheel, half-frozen, with water glistening on his bare head and oozing from his pale eyes.

chapter Thirteen
Down in the Forest Something Stirs again

Simpkin Sampkins was following the typhoon trail through the forest. He had been tracking it for hours, scrambling over toppled trees and hooking himself on splinters, and he was worn out. But still he kept going, because he was a man on a mission.

Simpkin was a very unhappy man, though. He was unhappy because by trying for once to be a hero instead of a fool, he had led the entire village to see his walking wood and so he had caused Tilly and the grolyhoomp to run away.

Now there was a curious thing, Simpkin thought. He had no idea what a grolyhoomp was and couldn't understand a word it said, but he had liked the look of it very much. He had enjoyed its smile and its sing-songy humming voice, and the warm way it looked at you when it was trying to understand you.

Simpkin was not surprised that the grolyhoomp had failed in its attempt to understand *him*, because he couldn't understand himself.

Mostly, though, Simpkin Sampkins liked the grolyhoomp because Tilly so obviously liked it too.

Yet he had caused it to be stoned and chased away.

He was determined to make up for that mistake, and he also had to warn Tilly about the fate that the Baron and her father were cooking up for her.

He was desperate to *save* her from it.

Simpkin had no idea how he was going to achieve this, but there was no point in worrying about that yet. He had to find Tilly first.

So on he ploughed, over tree and under bush and through the tearing briars.

At last he could go no further. His exhausted legs gave way and he collapsed on a mess of squashed toadstools and hung his head between his knees.

He did not know how long he had been sitting there – he thought he might have fallen asleep – when suddenly a sound made him wide awake.

By this time it was almost dark.

Simpkin had no idea where he was, but that did not worry him because he knew the forest better than anybody and he was sure he could find his way out of it.

What *did* worry him was the whispering.

It came skittering like a little breeze among the dead leaves under his feet. It hummed in the new green leaves over his head. And it came from somewhere very near.

Silent as a poacher – which of course he was –
Simpkin crept towards the sound.

The branches of a fallen tree spread in front of
him like a hedge. Softly – so quietly that he could
have caught an unsuspecting rabbit in his bare
hands – Simpkin moved the leaves aside.

This is what he saw.

On the other side of the tree there was a clearing
in the forest. In the clearing, in the dim evening
light, the grolyhoomp was sitting. Lying on his arm
was Tilly.

She was looking anxiously at the grolyhoomp's
stripy face and whispering, and he was humming
gently back at her.

Now Tilly reached down and scooped up some
soil, then reached up and rubbed it over the
grolyhoomp's face.

'One of your problems, George,' Simpkin heard
her saying, 'is that you have a luminous face. Your
enemies will see you a mile off. This will make that
harder.'

'Enn-emm-eyys,' said George. 'Ha-a-rrr-dd-
errr.'

'Exactly. Another trouble is, you're the wrong
size. I mean, you're probably the right size for a
grolyhoomp, but around here you stand out a bit.'

'S-t-a-an-dut.'

'Nearly.'

Tilly picked up some more soil, spat on it and kneaded it in her fingers. Then she flung the mud at George's forehead, where it stuck like a small currant on a large cake. She regarded him seriously.

'Have you any idea what I'm doing this for?'

George shook his head.

Listening to this made Simpkin Sampkins feel so guilty that he wanted to stick himself back in jail. But he dared not make a sound, so he stayed crouching in the undergrowth with leaves up his nose and his legs starting to cramp.

'What am I going to do with you?' Tilly murmured, smearing George's enormous nose. 'Everybody wants to hurt you just because you're different. And I'm in trouble too, so what are you going to do with me? What are we going to do with each other?'

George was quiet. He seemed to be miles away.

'You're not paying attention, are you?' said Tilly. 'Here, George, look at this.'

From the depths of her skirt she produced a small, battered but brightly polished spoon, and waved it in front of his face.

She might as well have been waving a matchstick at a tree. George squinted at the tiny shiny thing.

'Ymmylllochmidtilly? What's that?'

'This,' Tilly explained, 'is a spoon. You use it for eating. But you can also use it to see yourself. It's metal – very precious. It's my treasure, see?'

'Tttrrree-eee-szerrr.'

'You're catching on.' Tilly breathed on the spoon and rubbed it with her sleeve, as she had done every day for years. 'This is my mirror, George. Here, have a look and see what I've been doing to you.'

She held up the spoon in front of George's face.

He smiled, looking at her instead.

'Of course,' said Tilly, 'you look a bit twisted in a spoon. Staring into water is best, but you can't carry water in your pocket, can you? Go on then, look at yourself.'

George closed his eyes for a moment. He was beginning to feel very tired. It was a long, long time since he had last been asleep.

Tilly shook her head. 'I can see you're not interested, but one day you will be. So you can have my treasure. It's a present.'

George made no effort to take it, so Tilly pushed it into a pouch as big as a cave in his tunic. 'There, George. From my pocket to yours. Because we're friends.'

'Fffrrenndss.'

They grinned at each other.

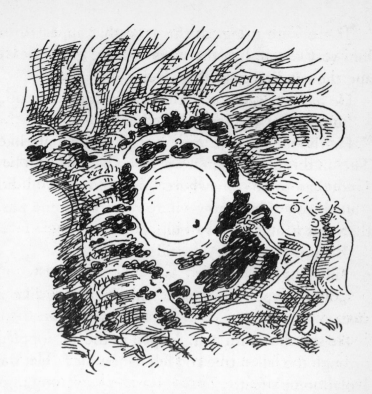

'I wonder what you think of us?' Tilly sighed. 'I wonder what you think of England? Not much, I expect, after today.'

But George was thinking something very different. He was thinking that perhaps the trouble was simply that he did not know these people enough yet to understand them. There had to be a reason why they grew angry and shouted and threw things, and laughed or cried at the drop of a hat. It was just that so far he could not see it.

There were things in this land that appealed to him very much, like the trees and the green fields and the winding sparkling river.

He had liked the crow that sat on his head, too.

But most of all George liked Tilly.

He thought that if there were more people like Tilly in this place, then it was not a bad place to be. If you had to be somewhere – as of course you did – and if you didn't know where your real home was, then this would do very well.

'E-nn-g-ll-a-nn-d,' he said softly.

Tilly laughed.

Cramp gripped Simpkin Sampkins's leg like a vice.

He shrieked with pain, leaped in the air, toppled through the fallen tree and fell flat on his face at the grolyhoomp's feet.

chapter Fourteen
The Star Man

In the Year of Our Lord 1103 people's lives were shorter, so they hurried things up a bit. For example, they married at a much younger age than they do now.

Even so, Tilly Miller considered that she was far too young to think about marriage. And it was her belief that even if she had been alive a thousand years, it would still be too soon to let herself be hitched to a stinking, scaly, scrawny dragon like Bones Lousewort.

That was why, when the three of them had got over the surprise of meeting like that in the middle of the dusky forest, and Simpkin had told her the Baron's vile plan, she began to think long and hard about what she could do.

Only one idea came to her.

'I could ask the Baron for mercy,' she said.

Simpkin Sampkins shook his head.

'That's a waste of time, Tilly. People like the Baron make rules to suit themselves. They love power and they *never* have mercy.'

Tilly sighed. 'Then what can I do?'

'You could ask your father to change his mind,' Simpkin suggested. 'He *is* your dad, after all.'

'He doesn't act like it, does he?' she said mournfully. 'But it's worth a try. I'll ask him in the morning – it's too late to go back now.'

Simpkin agreed, and soon he and Tilly had settled themselves against the grolyhoomp's side and closed their eyes to get some sleep.

George did not sleep. It was still not his time for rest, although he could feel it coming closer.

With his friends quiet, he lay back and looked up at the sky.

Once again, as on the night he arrived, stars shone down through the forest canopy.

Slowly the galaxies wheeled through their courses.

Shooting stars swooped.

And once again, so deep inside his ears that the sound might have been coming from his own head, George heard the universe singing.

Tilly was not asleep either.

Lying close to George, she could sense his excitement. She felt his arms tremble, heard his great heart beat faster.

She looked up and saw how intently he was scanning the sky. In the starlight his eyes glittered.

Then slowly his arm rose, with a finger outstretched. Up and up his arm reached, up and on until the finger had cleared the topmost branches and was pointing at ...

At what? Tilly couldn't tell.

George's arm stayed raised for a long time. Then Tilly felt his body heave a sigh. His arm withdrew and his finger folded in, and he was still again.

Tilly tugged at Simpkin's sleeve.

'W-wha-what is it?' the poacher stammered, startled from a dream of rabbit stew.

'Could you lead us past the mill in the dark?' Tilly whispered.

'Am I the poacher of poachers or am I not?' asked Simpkin. 'And hasn't this grolyhoomp left a track like a highway? Of course I could.'

'Good. Because I want us to go back now,' Tilly said. 'I want to see a man.'

'What man?'

'The star man.'

Simpkin gasped. 'The star man is a crazy man!'

'I want to see him anyway,' Tilly said, in a determined voice that left no room for arguing. 'Can we go now, please? We haven't much time.'

She nudged the grolyhoomp.

'Come on, Georgie, we're going. But move quietly, please. Try not to flatten the whole forest.'

The star man lived in a lonely mud-roofed hovel in the middle of an upland heath which rose swiftly beyond the mill. Gorse and bracken and heather stretched away on all sides as far as you could see.

Tilly had always thought this a very boring landscape, but that did not bother the star man. All he was interested in was the sky, and the night sky at that.

He was a long, lanky fellow with a straggly white beard and a habit of talking to himself. He hardly ever spoke to anybody *but* himself, for the simple reason that whenever anybody was about he was looking upwards and didn't see them.

So far as people could tell – and they did tell, making up new stories about him every day – the star man never ate and never washed and spent his life with his head sticking out of his roof, talking to the sky. So they said he was mad.

But the star man wasn't mad at all. He was just ahead of his time.

Mad or not, Tilly wanted to see him. And she wanted George to see him, crazy though that also seemed.

Because Tilly had a crazy idea.

Simpkin went along because he liked her company and was determined to protect her from harm if he could.

But he was afraid.

It was still dark when they arrived at the hovel on the heath, and the stars were still shining.

As they approached, they saw the star man's head poking out of the roof. He was gazing up in a dreamy sort of way and muttering what sounded like a spell.

'Gemini Cassiopeia Betelgeuse Orion Jupiter Mars.'

The words floated down to them on the night air, fluted in a high, piping, sing-songy voice as reverently as if they were holy scripture.

The sound frightened Simpkin witless.

But to Tilly it sounded like music and it sounded like poetry, even though, like grolyhoomp language, it made no actual sense.

She coughed to attract the stargazer's attention.

'Excuse me, sir.'

Startled, he let his eyes rove the starlit heath until they rested on a small girl and a bald man and the unbelievable bulk of George.

'Great suns in the universe,' he cried, 'what's that?'

'Please, Mr Star Man,' said Tilly, 'this is George. He's a grolyhoomp, and he wants –'

'He's a *what*?'

'A grolyhoomp, sir. I found him – or he found me – and he – no, we – that is, we have a question.'

'A question? A *question*? You want to ask me a *question*?'

The star man grew instantly excited. 'You mean you're *interested?* Well, that is wonderful. Wonderful. That is truly the most wondrous thing. Nobody ever wants to ask me a question. Nobody has asked me a question in years. And I *like* being asked questions, I *long* for it. Hold on, don't go away!'

The head disappeared and there was a crash as if he had fallen off a chair.

'This is madness,' Simpkin Sampkins moaned. 'I can't believe I'm part of it.'

The door of the hovel creaked open and the stargazer appeared, limping. He hobbled towards them. Twitching his beard like an exotic bird ruffling its feathers, he looked warily at Tilly, sharply at Simpkin Sampkins and astoundedly at George.

Since it was impossible to view George all at once, the star man examined him bit by bit, working up from his boots.

As he did so, his expression changed.

The sharpness vanished. The wariness disappeared.

Instead, as his eyes roved on and up over the huge trunk and the gigantic shoulders and the neck that went on for ever, there entered into them a look of wonder.

When he arrived at George's striped head it became a look of awe. Because from his point of view George's head appeared to be in the sky.

Starlight shone upon it. It was surrounded by twinkling lights. It was part of the universe. And most amazing of all, it shone itself, like a grubby star somebody had thrown mud at.

I am a star man, the stargazer was thinking, but this is a man of stars – if he is man at all, which I doubt. The girl says he's a grolyhoomp, and a grolyhoomp he may very well be. Whatever he is, I'm glad to have seen him. This is the very greatest moment of my life.

He blinked and swallowed and tried not to cry, but the thought that this miracle wanted to ask him a question was too much.

'He wants *my* opinion!' he sobbed. 'He has come to *me*!'

It was almost too much to bear.

'Oh!' he cried. 'Ask away! Ask me that question!'

Tilly nudged George. 'Go on, George, ask him,' she whispered. And she looked up at the sky.

'What's that supposed to mean?' cried Simpkin.

'George knows,' said Tilly.

To Simpkin's surprise, George appeared to understand. Slowly his arm lifted and stretched like unending elastic.

A finger unfolded and pointed deep into the blue-black, speckled bowl of the sky.

Simpkin closed his eyes. He could not believe what he was seeing, and preferred not to. It was too scary.

But the star man was so excited that he took the wonder of George's never-ending arm in his stride. He hurried round to where he could gaze up the long line of arm and pointing finger, dimly lit by the glow from George's face.

The star man drew in his breath. 'Is that the question?'

'Yes, that's the question,' Tilly said. 'At least, I think it is. Can you answer it?'

'Certainly I can,' the star man said confidently. 'Do you know, I am *glad* to be asked this question. In fact I am happy to be asked *any* question. I'm *here* to be asked questions, though nobody bothers. It's very frustrating.'

'Answer it then, please,' said Tilly politely.

'Well,' said the star man, 'if your friend is asking the question I think he's asking, he wants me to tell him what he's pointing at. And my reply is that he is pointing at the constellation of Ursa Middling.'

'Ursa what?'

'Ursa Middling. It lies halfway between the constellations of Ursa Major, or the Great Bear, and Ursa Minor, or the Little Bear. But further back.'

'How far back?' asked Tilly.

'Much further back,' said the star man. 'So much further that only I have seen it.'

'Is it far from here?'

The star man nodded. 'It is so far that it is for ever,' he said. 'For ever and ever and ever, that is how far it is.'

'Is there any way of getting there from here?' asked Tilly. 'Or to here from there?'

'That is the best joke I ever heard,' said the star man, though his smile was rather sad.

'Well, thank you very much,' said Tilly. 'We won't bother you any more.'

'Any time,' said the star man. 'I enjoyed that. Any time you think of a question, come and ask it. Ask me another. I like questions.'

Mumbling to himself, he limped back inside. The door creaked shut.

Tilly felt disappointed. She had been hoping for more. But maybe more was impossible to get.

'What was that all about?' Simpkin asked as they picked their way down from the heath towards the shining river below.

'I don't know,' replied Tilly. 'And I don't think George knows either. But I'm sure it was about *something*.'

'Well, that clears it up,' Simpkin said.

Then he nodded towards a faint light that was beginning to show in the eastern sky.

'Here's another something, Tilly. You're getting married today.'

Chapter Fifteen
Trick or Treat

Nobody was allowed to sleep in Castle Lousewort that night, for the Baron had commanded that everything be made ready for the immediate marriage of his glorious son Bones to Tilly Miller. It was to be the grandest of weddings.

Messengers were dispatched far and wide to invite guests from all corners of the countryside.

The castle musicians were ordered to rehearse their most rousing wedding music.

The cooks in the kitchens were charged to produce the tastiest wedding fare ever tasted.

The maids were commanded to scour the castle from top to bottom and then scrub it all over again, until not a speck of dust remained and everything gleamed so brightly that it made your eyes hurt.

The grooms were required to polish the wedding carriage until they could see their faces in it more clearly than in a mirror.

The result of all these commands was that everyone ran round in a panic and got in everybody else's way.

And the bridegroom?

Well.

Bones Lousewort was getting nervous.

'Do you think this is such a good idea after all,

Dad?' he squeaked as a bevy of barbers snipped and shampooed his hair into curls and manicured his nails and massaged his cheeks until they were redder than a reindeer's nose. 'Am I not too young?'

'Too young?' yodelled the Baron, admiring his new wig in a pewter mirror so dull it made him look almost presentable. 'How can you be too young? Listen, Bones, do you want Tilly or not?'

'Of course I do. But –'

'I don't want any buts. It's lucky for you her father is such a greedy guzzler and I have the money to satisfy him. So be happy, my boy, be happy! I'm preparing for you a wedding feast you wouldn't believe!'

Bones smiled. He felt reassured. There was nothing he liked better than getting his own way, especially when someone *persuaded* him to have it.

The Baron smiled too. This wig was magic, he thought. It would do wonders for him at the feast. Those country ladies would think him the handsomest baron in the world. He was almost happy.

Almost.

There was one cloud on the Baron's horizon. The grolyhoomp.

He had felt uneasy about that strange creature

ever since it had seemed to look right through him. Try as he might, he could not get it out of his mind.

That was why he had commanded his steward and bailiff to get rid of the beast permanently, once and for all and for ever. They were seeing to it right now.

Afterwards there would be no grolyhoomp and no clouds anywhere.

The Baron heaved a sigh of satisfaction.

'I think of everything,' he said out loud. 'I'm marvellous!'

Silas Sludge and Bartholomew Bog were also pleased with themselves, because they had worked out a foolproof plan for geting rid of the grolyhoomp.

They were going to murder him.

They were going to kill him with poison.

Reasoning that George must be getting hungry, they had prepared an enormous platter loaded with every kind of meat, sweetmeat, vegetable, cake and biscuit known to man in the Year of Our Lord 1103.

It looked tempting. It smelled irresistible. It was mouth-watering and scrumptious.

But inside the food, Silas and Bartholomew had hidden every kind of poison known to man in the

Year of Our Lord 1103, from hemlock and deadly nightshade to poison ivy and the venom of toadstools.

Chuckling with happiness and staggering under its weight, they carried the dish to the edge of the forest across the river from the mill.

'This will blow that grolyhoomp's belly sky high,' chortled the Sludge. 'I'm glad I thought of it.'

'It will toast his tonsils. It will grill his gizzard. I'm glad *I* thought of it,' the Bog sniggered.

'No, *you* thought of it.'

'Not at all, *you* did.'

Laughing at their triumph, they placed the platter under a tree above the beach, and retired to watch.

It looked like a picnic.

Soon after this, Tilly and her companions arrived at the mill.

While the others waited outside, Tilly went in to ask the miller to let her off the wedding.

'Please, Father,' she begged, 'I don't want to be married.'

'Tell me you're joking,' he replied jovially. 'Why ever not?'

'Because I don't like Bones,' Tilly said.

The miller gaped at her. 'You don't?'

'I can't stand him. His breath chokes me.'

'Well, hit me with a corncrake,' her father snapped, growing angry now. 'What has that got to do with it? Who cares what you like? You'll do as you're told, my girl, or else! Believe me, marrying Bones will be a walk in the park compared to what will happen to you if you don't.'

Tilly began to cry, but her tears had no effect on the rock-hard miller. Twisting her hair with trembling fingers, she sobbed, 'I'll hang myself!'

'Not until I have my five gold coins, you won't,' growled the miller. 'You can do as you like afterwards.'

'I'll run away then,' Tilly cried.

'Where to?' the miller shouted. 'Where would you go? For miles and miles there's nothing but wolves and wildcats and tusked boars. You'd be breakfast before you got five miles.'

But he tied Tilly's hands just in case, and roped her to her bed.

Outside, morning was breaking. Mist rolled up the river. There was a hint of rain to come.

Simpkin Sampkins snored beside the water-wheel, dreaming of mermaids. They were flicking water at him with their tails, and he loved them in his sleep.

George, hungry and thirsty, sucked water from the river.

As he drank, a delicious smell wafted across his nostrils and made his stomach twist inside him. He had eaten nothing since the crash and he had never felt so hungry.

Following the scent, he forded the river and sniffed his way to the line of trees where he saw a platter heaped with food, lying under the branches as if it was waiting for him.

He was too hungry to ask questions.

Picking up the platter in one hand, he leaned back his head and tipped the food into his mouth, soup, nuts and piecrust.

Silas Sludge and Bartholomew Bog watched him from their hiding place. They patted each other on the back. What a wonderful idea they'd had! In no time the grolyhoomp would be history.

Laughing and skipping they headed back towards Castle Lousewort to tell the Baron that his troubles were over.

There was nothing to stop the wedding now.

chapter Sixteen
The Sacrificial Bride

At six o'clock in the morning, when it was still not fully light, a carriage arrived at the mill.

From it stepped six sleepy maids, each carrying equipment designed to transform a humble miller's daughter into a bride fit for a baron's son to marry.

One maid carried a golden wedding dress.

Another carried golden underwear.

A third bore a silken cushion on which stood a pair of golden shoes, sparkling with precious stones.

The fourth maid held high a golden comb to dress the bride's hair and a diamond tiara to adorn it.

The fifth brought a box padded with silk, containing jars of the finest perfumes of Araby.

The sixth maid lugged a casket studded with

rubies and stuffed with half a hundredweight of jewels, to hang round Tilly's throat and waist and wrists and ankles.

When he heard the carriage approaching, Simpkin Sampkins squeezed himself into the niche in the wall supporting the waterwheel. He lay there curled up and trembling like a sodden mouse in a very wet hole and watched with awe this parade of attendants led by a fat coachman with a squint.

The coachman hammered his fist on the mill door.

Inside the mill, the noise rattled the roof timbers and sent dust falling down in streams. Rats scuttled into their holes. Spiders fled to the furthest corners of their webs.

The miller opened the door and with cringing respect scraped the ground with his head as the maids paraded by.

'Up the stairs, my beauties,' he wheedled, 'go on up, my daughter eagerly awaits you. Do what you like with her.'

When she saw them coming with all this finery, Tilly cried, 'Take it away! I don't want any of it! You'll make me look like a princess and I don't want to be a princess! I don't want to be the Baron's daughter-in-law! I don't want to be married at all!'

Nobody took any notice.

The maids did what they had been commanded to do.

They doused Tilly in freezing water, scrubbed her thoroughly and anointed her with the perfumes of Araby.

They dressed her in the golden underwear and the golden dress.

They brushed her hair till it shone with a golden sheen, and fastened in it the golden comb and dazzling diamond tiara.

They put silk stockings on her legs and fitted the sparkling shoes on her feet.

Lastly they fastened a necklace of rubies round her throat, a belt of silver about her waist, and jewelled bracelets on her wrists and ankles.

Then they held up a mirror so that she could see herself.

Tilly wept.

'I'm not Tilly Miller any more,' she sobbed. 'I'm a sacrifice!'

Now she was dragged kicking and screaming from the mill, lifted on top of the carriage and made to sit there in full view of all the people she would pass on her momentous journey.

For the carriage was to make a triumphal progress about the countryside and then parade through the village to the church where the bridegroom would be waiting.

The Baron had decreed that *everybody* was to see the bride on her wedding day.

Now Tilly could scream her head off and nobody would hear her, because in front of the carriage there marched sixteen trumpeters in scarlet livery, and the sound of their trumpets split the air and made the birds fly off in fright.

As the carriage rolled away, the miller brushed a tear of joy from his eye. He thought he might raise his daughter's price because she looked so beautiful.

As the carriage left the mill yard, Simpkin Sampkins squeezed out of his mouse hole. Wringing water from his clothes and shaking it from his ears, he sighed bitterly to see Tilly looking so lovely, only to be wasted on a ninny like Bones Lousewort.

Simpkin followed the procession at a safe distance, and wondered if there was anything that anyone could do to save Tilly from her fate.

But in his heart he knew there was not. The Baron was too powerful.

And as the carriage began its fateful journey, across the river George blinked at the light filtering down into the cool shade of the forest.

Looking over the water, he thought he saw a carriage leaving the mill with an angel sitting on top, but he could not be certain.

George could not be certain of anything any more.

Because now his waking time was really up. He was already half-asleep. His limbs were sluggish and growing heavier every minute. It was time for him to be in bed.

But there was something else as well.

Something worse.

Something terrible.

There was pain.

The pain was like nothing George had ever felt before.

He felt sick, and every part of his body hurt.

Shivers of agony shot through his arms and legs

and sped like arrows up his neck, where they changed into hammers to beat his skull. His stomach had swelled like a gigantic balloon, and it was still rising. Torture was going on in there.

George rubbed his eyes and blinked and squinted. He could hardly see for drowsiness and pain.

Was it Tilly sitting on top of that carriage disappearing around the bend of the river, or was it not?

Was that her voice he could hear?

If it was, was she crying?

With grolyhoompian effort he struggled to his knees and rocked there, wheezing and groaning.

The trees held hands and swung round him in a ring.

They began to move more quickly – faster and faster until they whirled like a tornado.

And slowly, slowly, slowly, like a tree falling in slow motion, George toppled forward, rolled over on his back and lay still.

The spring weather had changed in the night. There was a dampness in the air.

Now, very gently, with a touch as soft as feathers, rain began to fall.

The drops made circles on the river.

They whispered on the leaves above George's head.

And feathers of rain drifted down on his unconscious face, on and on.

chapter Seventeen
A Wedding Like No Other

Two hours after setting out, at the end of a triumphant procession along a route lined with cheering peasants waving flags and flowers (they had been ordered by the Baron to applaud or else), Tilly finally arrived at the church for her wedding.

The church was a small, simple wooden building set in a green field below the rocky hill on which the Baron's castle stood.

The priest, chubby and smiling, waited at the door while the bride was helped down from the carriage.

It was raining hard now and everyone except Tilly was very wet. All through the journey the maids had leaned out of the carriage doors to hold umbrellas of plaited sackcloth and grass over Tilly's head, keeping her dry while they themselves got soaked to the skin.

They were not happy about this.

Nor was the miller, who, dripping steadily, was waiting outside the church to lead his daughter up the aisle to her bridegroom.

Simpkin Sampkins, squelching along behind the procession, was oozing rain from every pore. It seemed to Simpkin that he had spent days getting wetter and wetter, and that if this went on any longer he would turn into a fish.

Inside the crowded church the bridegroom and his father were dry but growing impatient.

The Baron wore his brightest suit of armour and looked very manly and splendid.

Bones, on the other hand, had been dressed up like Tilly.

He wore a tight, white, choking ruff around his scrawny neck, a scarlet jerkin, short, puffy, blue trousers and a pair of long, yellow tights which clung like a second skin to his bandy legs.

Bones looked a twerp, but a dangerous twerp.

He had a nasty gleam in his eye, and since he had feasted on garlic for breakfast, his breath was more fearsome than ever. Some weaker guests unfortunate enough to be within whiffing range had fainted away, and lay flopped over their pews or in heaps on the floor. Every time they came to, another breath from Bones knocked them out again.

Only the Baron seemed immune, but that was probably because he smelled even worse himself.

At last a bright halloo of trumpets was heard outside, and the church door swung open. The trumpeters marched slowly in, followed by other musicians.

'Father!' Bones gasped in a fit of nervous excitement. 'Oh, Father!'

The Baron slapped him on the back. 'This is your hour, my boy,' he laughed. 'Now's your time!'

They watched eagerly as the procession moved at a stately pace up the church. Musicians, trumpeters, choirboys, pageboys and maids of honour all followed each other, like the animals entering Noah's Ark, two by two.

They were all dressed in the grandest finery, but even so, nothing prepared Bones for the vision of his golden bride.

Tilly clung nervously to her father's arm, but even though she was pale and terrified, she still looked glorious.

Bones's heart flipped inside his meagre chest. 'Ahh!' he cried, heaving a sigh which felled four rows of the congregation. He swaggered into the aisle to greet his bride.

Tilly would not look at him.

The miller pushed her towards Bones, and Bones took her soft fingers in his skeletal fist, but still she would not look at him.

'Look at your bridegroom, Tilly,' said the priest.

But she would not.

'Look at my son, you ungrateful little beast!' the Baron hissed.

But Tilly would not. Instead she turned her face as far away from him as she could.

Bones stamped his foot. 'Look at me, Tilly,' he pleaded. 'If you don't, I shall get in a temper, and I'm not nice in a temper. You wouldn't like it.'

Still Tilly refused to look anywhere near him. She was shaking from head to toe and her eyes had filled with tears at the thought of all the freedom and adventure she might have had but would never get now.

The congregation began to grow restless. They started to whisper to each other and hiss.

'For heaven's sake, look at him, Tilly Miller!'

'Look at Bones!'

'Smile at your bridegroom.'

'Whatever you do, don't put him in a temper.'

'Please don't make the Baron angry, or we'll all suffer.'

'Oh, look, Tilly, for heaven's sake!'

'Look! Look!'

The hisses grew to a shout, and the shout swelled to a roar, and the roar raised the timbers of the church roof, which was quite flimsy.

Tilly shut her ears and tried not to hear any of it. 'I hate them,' she told herself. 'All they can think about is themselves, so I hate them all!'

The noise was extraordinary.

The trumpets brayed.

The viols screeched.

The people screamed and shouted.

The rain hissed down outside.

There was a rattle of thunder.

Altogether there was such a din that nobody heard the strange new sounds enter in.

There was a sound of creaking.

There was a sound of wrenching.

There was a sound of splitting.

Nobody realised what was happening until half the church roof disappeared and rain poured inside on to the heads of the wedding guests.

Then all noises stopped at once.

As one man the entire congregation looked up and saw a grolyhoomp looking down.

The rain had woken George from his sleep-sodden torpor.

He had squeezed rain from his eyes, licked it from his lips and wiped it from his face.

He had gripped his bloated belly to still the pains that writhed in it like snakes.

Then he had heard music.

Somewhere a long way off, trumpets were playing. High and shrieking, they sounded like a girl's screams.

Was it Tilly?

George remembered her cries on the carriage.

What was happening to her?

Like a drunken man he had pushed himself to his feet and staggered towards the noise. Across the countryside he reeled like a sick giraffe.

At last, tired and tormented to distraction by the devils inside him, he arrived at the church. He heard the trumpets inside. The viols. The shouting. He understood none of it.

But then, deep inside the din, he heard Tilly crying.

George understood that. He understood that inside this building something terrible was happening to his friend. But he could not see what it was.

So he raised the roof.

For a moment everyone inside the church was speechless, except Tilly.

'George!' she cried. 'Oh, George!'

George was trying to take it in, but the film of sleep kept slipping over his eyes and the snakes were wriggling along his arms and legs and up his neck into his head, making him giddy.

Through the film and the snakes he looked down at Tilly.

'G-ee-o-o-r-r-g-g-e,' he said. 'Ff-orrt-i-ff-y!'

To the people in the church this sounded like a rallying cry. 'Fortify yourselves!' they thought the grolyhoomp was saying. 'Fortify yourselves against this evil baron and his reeking son, who keep you in poverty and make your lives a misery! Shake off the yoke that has made you their slaves. Fight them!'

'Ff-orrr-ti-ffy,' said George again.

He hardly knew what he was doing. Blinking and

squeezing his eyes, he tossed away the roof timbers and probed down a finger.

Bones thought the finger was coming to get him. He yelled with fright and ran to hide behind the altar.

But Tilly knew the finger was coming for her. She grabbed hold of it and George lifted her right out of the church.

When he saw his son's bride soar into the air, the Baron's face swelled like an overripe pomegranate.

Speechless with rage, he beckoned to his steward and bailiff, and when they crept close, sweating with fear, he swiped them off their feet with two blows of his fists.

Then he signalled to his trumpeters to play the fighting fanfare.

This fanfare was a pre-arranged signal. The day he came to power, the Baron had laid plans to protect his lands and castle if ever they should be threatened by an enemy. Now those plans were to be put into practice.

The fanfare was a message to the Baron's troops.

It was a call to battle.

It was a declaration of war.

Inside the castle, as soon as they heard the silvery squeal echo faintly from the valley below, the

Baron's soldiers gathered their weapons and leaped on their horses.

All the machinery of war, for attack and defence, was made ready in double-quick time.

With a deafening clanking of chains, a drawbridge was lowered over the slimy, stinking moat that surrounded the castle.

And out of the castle, over the drawbridge, into the unsuspecting world, there rode the Baron's invincible army.

chapter Eighteen
Into Battle

The people ran from the church prepared to rally to the grolyhoomp's cry and rise up against their oppressors.

But when they looked towards Castle Lousewort they changed their minds.

This is what they saw.

They saw a hundred horsemen clad in chain mail riding down the steep slope towards them. Each horseman carried an axe and a sword and a spear and rode high upon an armoured steed.

Behind them the wedding guests saw more horses and riders pulling enormous catapults and hauling cauldrons of boiling oil that steamed and hissed in the rain.

Behind those they saw two hundred footsoldiers

pushing a battering ram made from the biggest tree that ever grew in the forest.

The people saw flags waving and pennants flying and armour flashing, and they saw the snorting nostrils of the horses.

They saw Death marching towards them down the hill.

These people were simple and unarmed and unprotected, and the sight scared them silly. They were so terrified that they climbed over each other to hide behind the church for shelter.

The Baron and Bones, followed at a ragged trot by Silas and Bartholomew, jumped on their horses and galloped to ride at the head of their army.

From its leading rider the Baron snatched his great flag embroidered with the Lousewort arms, a scarlet dragon breathing fire. He shook it furiously and roared vengeance on the grolyhoomp and every person in Lousewort land who had the nerve to stand at his side.

The Baron was a terrifying sight.

Bones was less so. He rode behind his father, keeping out of the way.

And the rain rained down.

When the soldiers reached the bottom of the hill, they fanned out into a line and advanced steadily. Right in the middle was the battering ram, and on each side of this there rolled a catapult loaded with boiling oil.

Forward they came. Forward and onward, closer and closer.

George screwed up his eyes at the sight of the approaching army. It was all very hazy, but even so he was fairly sure that these people were not friendly.

He was still holding Tilly in his fist.

Tilly no longer looked like a princess or a bride. Her hair dripped, her tiara hung askew, her dress was smudged and torn and she had lost her golden shoes.

'George!' she cried anxiously. 'They want to kill you. You must protect yourself – you'll have to flee!'

'Grolyhoomp,' George answered.

He tried to smile at her but a terrible cramp was gripping his stomach and the smile didn't come out right.

It looked like a frightening lunatic grimace.

The nearest of the Baron's horsemen saw it and trembled. This was the first time most of them had seen the grolyhoomp that everyone was talking about, and it was even worse than they had imagined.

They looked at the colossal mound of his belly and quaked, for it was *still* swelling. It was growing so enormous that now they could hardly see what lay above it. Then suddenly George's ostrich neck and head were hidden from view altogether.

'Heaven knows what's going on up there,' the horsemen groaned.

The Baron's army halted, twenty paces from the grolyhoomp.

George reached out his arm and put Tilly gently

down behind the wall of the church with the rest of the congregation.

'Stay there,' he said in his own language. 'Fyjkvoatkif eishnnmufpikel.'

Simpkin Sampkins put his arm around Tilly. 'I'll look after you, my girl,' he said.

'Poor George,' Tilly whispered. 'Poor George.'

The Baron and George looked at each other.

'Go away, ugliness,' the Baron sneered. 'This is your last chance.'

'Fortify,' said George. And he belched.

Now a grolyhoomp belch is an awesome thing. It blew the helmet clean off the Baron's head and the flag from his hand.

The catapult captains saw the flag falling and took this to be their signal to action. At a single barked command, the heavy horses winched back the huge hammers.

The catapults creaked and trembled under the strain.

Their wheels nearly lifted off the ground.

The cauldrons teetered.

'Look out, George!' Tilly screamed, running from her shelter to stand at George's feet.

'Leave him alone!' she shouted to the Baron. 'Five hundred to one isn't fair!'

Simpkin Sampkins, with more courage than he

had ever dreamed he possessed, scuttled out like a frantic crab, snatched Tilly and dragged her back behind the church.

Just in time.

The catapult captains shouted their command.

'Fire fire!'

Immediately soldiers tossed flaming torches into the cauldrons to set the oil alight.

Axes cut off ropes.

The flaming cauldrons were catapulted into the air, spraying molten fiery fat in all directions.

At that moment a bell clanged inside George's brain.

Far away, on his world in the constellation of Ursa Middling, a day the length of nine hundred Earth years had ended and an evening curfew was tolling the citizens to their beds.

The curfew had tolled for so long that it had become like a bell ringing deep inside their heads to send them into trance-like sleep.

No one could resist.

And although George was light years away, the bell still rang in his ears, and he could not resist it either. His eyes closed and he began to nod just as the cauldrons came sailing through the air towards him.

One whistled harmlessly past his ear.

The other hit him square on the chin, spitting scalding oil over his face and setting his beard alight.

George's eyes jerked open.

'Ow!' he cried, spinning away from the source of the pain.

'Bend down!' he heard Tilly screaming. 'Duck, George!'

Dimly he saw Tilly and Simpkin beside his feet,

waving their arms. Flames roared in his ears, making such a noise he could not hear what they were saying.

He bent right down to listen.

'Stay there,' Tilly cried. 'Don't move!'

Tilly and Simpkin and the villagers grabbed buckets from the church and raced to fill them from puddles the rain had made all over the field. Then they ran back and tossed the water into George's face.

His beard hissed as the water hit the flames. He spluttered and spat and sighed with relief.

In all this excitement George did not hear the captain of the battering ram shout, 'Forward!'

And because he was looking the other way he did not see the great ram, pushed by two hundred men, come trundling towards him.

Faster and faster it rolled.

Neither did George hear the Baron's command to 'Charge!', and he did not see the cavalry come galloping at him waving axes and swords and spears.

Tilly did.

She shouted a warning but it was too late.

The battering ram hit the crouching George on his backside.

The blow had a most unexpected effect.

The poisoned platter prepared by Silas Sludge and Bartholomew Bog had filled George with billowing poisonous gas. It was this that had blown him up like a balloon.

When he bent down to have his beard extinguished, George compressed the gas to danger level. He became a volcano ready to erupt.

The battering ram was the detonator. As *Crash!* the tree smacked into his rear, so *Crack!* with a noise like a thunderclap George exploded.

Afterwards nobody could remember exactly the order in which things happened next, because they all seemed to happen together.

At the explosion, George's tunic billowed outwards and a wind like a hurricane, stinking a hundred times worse than Bones Lousewort's breath, blew the batterers clean off their ram and the catapult men to kingdom come.

The stench caught Silas Sludge and Bartholomew Bog full blast and wiped them out in a whiff.

The gale tore through the horsemen and hurled them off their steeds. Coughing and spluttering, with their eyes streaming, they staggered blindly about.

In no time the Baron's entire army was reeling and gasping for fresh air.

A grolyhoomp passing wind is an awesome thing.

George himself felt a whole lot better. As the wind wafted across his enemies, he experienced a delicious relief. He rose to his full height and yelled, *'Grolyhoomp!'* with such gusto that it caused a second eruption.

That finished what the first had begun.

Everybody left standing in that invincible army, including the Baron and Bones, passed out on the spot.

Tilly clapped her hands.

'Hooray!' she shouted. 'Hooray for Big George!'

'Three cheers for the grolyhoomp!' yelled the villagers, who could hardly believe their eyes or their noses. 'Hip hip, hooray! Hip hip, hooray! Hip hip –'

They stopped in mid-cheer. They gasped, because something strange was happening to their saviour. Something ominous.

'Look!' they whispered. 'Look, his eyes are closing!'

George's eyes had shut tight. He was swaying from side to side and backwards and forwards and round and round. The triumphant smile seemed to have frozen on his face.

'George!' Tilly cried. 'George, what's the matter?'

Inside George's head the curfew was clanging hypnotically. Like a drum it was beating out the same message over and over.

'*Time to go to sleep,*' it insisted. '*Go to sleep, George. Sleep …*'

George leaned further and further backwards.

Tilly screamed.

'Look out!' yelled Simpkin Sampkins, and everybody ran for cover.

George toppled over.

He hit the ground with a force like an earthquake, and beneath his body the Baron, Bones, Sludge, Bog, the miller and half an army were flattened and buried six feet under.

chapter Nineteen
Goodnight, George

Never had England seen such an astonishing victory.

As George fell, the rain ceased, the storm clouds rolled away southward and the sun came out to shine warmly upon the field of battle.

But there was no celebration.

Tears rolled down Tilly's cheeks as she looked at her fallen champion and felt her heart breaking.

Simpkin Sampkins's watery eyes ran like the mill race.

The villagers doffed their hats in respect for the extraordinary saviour who had sacrificed his life to rid them of a tyrant. They looked at him sprawled on the ground and wondered how they were going to bury him.

It would take weeks to dig a big enough hole.

Then suddenly, with a heave of his enormous chest, George drew a deep breath and blew it out again in a snore like another hurricane.

'Hooray!' they all cried. 'Our great champion is alive! He isn't dead but only sleeping!'

Weeping for joy, Tilly gripped George's finger in her hands and whispered, 'My hero!'

Now they all waited for the grolyhoomp to wake up.

And waited.

They waited until it grew dark, and then they set watches through the night to guard their deliverer against marauding wolves.

They set them again the next night.

And the next.

Still they waited, and still George showed no sign of waking.

It seemed unbelievable, but no matter how much noise they made, or how hard they prodded him, he slept on like a dead man.

Days multiplied into weeks.

One by one the villagers gave up and returned to their homes.

Finally only Tilly Miller and Simpkin Sampkins were left.

Then even they had to give in.

Sadly they turned their backs on George.

Gradually life in the village returned to normal. That is, normal except for the fact that now there was no wicked Baron to bully them. Normal except for the grolyhoomp that lay snoring below the castle in the meadow beside the church.

Rain fell on him, and the wind and sun dried him again.

Everybody was sure that before long he would catch cold, or else the King's spies would come snooping and find him. Goodness knew what would happen to Big George then.

But what could they do about it?

It was Tilly's idea to make a shelter.

Building the shelter took months of labour and noise. George slept through it all.

It was Simpkin Sampkins's idea to make the shelter look like a hill, so that no one would suspect there was anything of interest inside.

So huge earth walls were raised on each side of the sleeping Stranger.

Tall trees were felled and hauled and planted like massive pit props, and over these a roof was spread.

Cunning holes, which could not be seen from the outside, allowed fresh air inside.

At first when the structure was complete, it resembled an enormous dome. But when the people had covered it with turf and sown flowers and shrubs and small trees, it really did look like a hill.

Tilly planted the last flower of all. She planted a wild briar rose and called it Big George.

Underneath the rose she buried a stone tablet. On it she had written, in old Anglo-Saxon so that no Norman conqueror would be able to read it, *'Here sleeps the biggest hero in the world.'*

The flowers of spring and summer, the falling leaves of autumn, the snows of winter came and went, and came and went again.

Big George slept on.

At Tilly's request, Simpkin Sampkins took over the running of the mill. He gave up poaching and looked after Tilly like his own true and much loved daughter, and they were very happy together.

Later, when she grew up, Tilly married and had

children of her own. Then her children had children, on and on, generation after generation.

And as the generations arrived and departed, gradually people forgot all about the hero under the hill.

Big George knew nothing about any of it. He slept quietly, settling deeper and deeper into his nine hundred years' rest.

All this happened a long time ago.

But although Tilly and the villagers faithfully kept the secret of the grolyhoomp so that George could remain undisturbed, with the passing years an extraordinary tale began to be whispered throughout the kingdom.

It told how in a remote village at the edge of a forest, a Stranger had rescued a beautiful girl from the clutches of a monster. With each telling the story grew, until the Stranger became a knight in shining armour and then a saint who had killed a dragon – a real dragon breathing fire.

And so a legend was born.

afterword

Three things remain to be said.

The first may concern you, and it is this.

As the centuries wheeled by, many of Tilly's descendants became travellers and settled across the world.

Today they are living at all points of the compass, north, south, east and west, anywhere and everywhere.

So wherever you are, it is possible that you may be one of them.

The second thing concerns Big George.

Because his secret was kept so well, all knowledge of his whereabouts faded from memory. Nobody now knows where he is, just as nobody ever knew just where he came from in the first place.

But he's somewhere around, peacefully sleeping inside a dome that looks like a hill. Perhaps it is that curious-looking hump near you.

Better go and take a closer look. See if it has a wild briar rose growing on it.

The third thing concerns both you and George, and it is this.

The inhabitants of a star hidden deep inside the constellation of Ursa Middling sleep for exactly nine hundred Earth years.

The events of this story happened nine hundred years ago, more or less.

You know what that means.

It means that unless something unexpected broke into his sleep and woke him early – always a possibility – then any moment now Big George will be waking up and bursting from his shelter like a chicken from an egg.

Some chicken!

Unless, of course, he is awake already.

And that means that any minute now you could see your first grolyhoomp. So keep your eyes peeled. You wouldn't want to miss Big George.

And who knows, you may even be in his next adventure.